Hey Guy,
This Is
The
Butterfly

Grace De Soto Ferry

Hey Guy, This Is The Butterfly
A collection of Short Stories, Tall Tales,
Some True, Some Not
by
GRACE DE SOTO FERRY

Cover image cropped and modified to black
and white from a color photograph
by Carol. M. Highsmith

LilliMar Pictures Press
PO Box 3185, Santa Barbara, CA 93130
www.LilliMar.com

For John,
whose inspiration,
encouragement, support and love, made
this book possible.

Contents

Acknowledgments - *5*

Foreword - *7*

Hey Guy, This Is The Butterfly - *9*

Passing For White - *13*

The Ladies - *19*

Jimmy - *31*

The One-Eyed Saint of Muddy Creek - *33*

The Green Dress - *39*

Someone Should Change the Sign - *41*

Black Moon Rising - *47*

Maybe You're a Gypsy Too - *53*

The Cat in the Window - *57*

Maids - *59*

Blessed Benny the Benevolent - *61*

Torquemada's Slipper or La Chancla - *71*

Love Me Tender - *73*

The Bench - *83*

My Short Career As a Witch - *85*

Hey, Ugly - *87*

The Unexpected - *93*

Lone Star Diner - *99*

Stardust Trailer Park - *105*

John Wayne Wears a Girdle - *117*

Tillie and Ted - *123*

I Remember the Alamo - *131*

Gone - *137*

Acknowledgments

Special thanks to Joan Fallert for her wisdom and encouragement, Shirley Diamond and Joyce Wieder for their invaluable assistance, Dina Castillo who encouraged me to go forward, Carol M. Highsmith for allowing me to use her wonderful photograph on the cover, and last but not least, to my husband, John, whose patience and hard work prepared this book for publication.

Foreword

In 1940 my father built our house on the corner of West Commerce and 29th. I lived here from the time I was born until I left San Antonio in 1962. The neighborhood was and continues to be predominantly Mexican.

Several things remain sharp in my mind. The house where I grew up; the pecan tree in the back yard; the smell of bread baking in the panaderia half a block away; and the bar across the street - Hey Guy, This is The Butterfly.

After fifty years I came back to San Antonio. The passage of time and what some call progress have changed the neighborhood beyond recognition. Where my house used to be is now a Burger King. Next door, my grandmother's house is gone, as well as many other places I remember. The Butterfly is gone too. All that remains is an empty, weed-choked lot surrounded by a chain-link fence.

The photograph on the cover is not The Butterfly. Carol M. Highsmith's photo (taken in San Antonio) is reminiscent of such places.

Hey Guy, This Is The Butterfly

"Hey, you stupid drunks, quit that fighting!" Strong words followed by a bucket of water from the upstairs window. The cold water was enough to sober them or at least stop the fight.

"Sorry, Anita," said one of the men looking up to where she was leaning out the second story window.

On hot nights we'd sit on our small porch, highway 90 ran between us and the bar called The Butterfly. Actually, its full name - Hey Guy, This Is The Butterfly - was painted across the entire front of the small building. How it got its name I never knew.

Anita dumping water on the drunks always made us laugh and we'd yell across the highway, "Good for you Anita, let'em have it!"

Joe ran the bar and Anita ran Joe and everything else. I admired her. A petite woman with bright eyes and wavy black hair. She wasn't afraid of the drunks. Anita and Joe lived above the bar; she was aware of all the goings on. If some guys got too loud she'd march down the back stairs, walk into the bar and tell them to shut up, unlike my mother who would risk crossing the highway just so she didn't have to share the sidewalk with any of the bar's patrons.

Anita and Joe were very different. Joe would send the drunks home in a taxi to make sure they didn't get run over trying to cross the highway and Anita would threaten and shout insults at them for being unruly.

They never had children of their own although they raised a baby girl. Her name was Isabel and she was older than me by a few years. I remember hearing the story of how late one night this baby was brought to Anita by a relative. The story went that the baby was neglected, dirty and hungry. Anita took her in. Isabel grew into a pretty girl, tall, slender with hazel eyes. She was friends with my older sister. Sometimes we'd sneak into the bar when it was closed, and we'd check the jukebox for nickels.

Anita had a soft side that she kept private. I remember a woman who worked as a barmaid, her name was Juanita. She was a big woman with a wonderful throaty laugh. She dressed in bright colors and wore flowers in her hair; she was not a pretty woman but all the men liked her. She had a little boy that came with her everywhere, even to the bar. Anita would bring him upstairs, feed him and let him sleep until Juanita was ready to go home.

The Butterfly had a jukebox and depending on the mood of the patrons we might hear happy norteño music or sad and sappy songs. Our favorites were always the mambos. When one came on the jukebox all us kids would jump off the porch and wiggle and shake our behinds like the dancers we'd seen in Mexican movies at The Alameda.

On those hot, sticky nights we'd sit on the porch waiting for a cool breeze. We'd see the men staggering out of the bar and we'd bet on which one would land in the bushes before he'd reach the corner. My mom and my aunt talked about better times and us kids counted the trucks on the highway.

Passing For White

The street is melting. I'm standing under a skinny tree watching car tires sink into the soft tar. It looks like licorice after I chew it and spit it out. Black and soft.

It's a short bus ride to town. I put a nickel in the metal box and listen to it clanging all the way down. I know I belong in the back but I plop my behind in a front seat next to an open window. I'm waiting for the driver to yell out, "To the back!" But he doesn't, it's too hot to fight with the riders.

I'm not going to do what the signs tell me. I'm going to drink water from both For Whites Only and For Colored Only fountains. I'm going to speak Spanish to the girl behind the counter at Kress' Five and Dime. She doesn't understand me. I don't care.

The drinking fountains at Woolworths are pink with pink tile on the wall. The soda fountain has stools that spin around. I can make myself dizzy. On the counter are signs in shiny metal frames that tell you where the White Section ends and the Colored Only begins. I sit on a stool right in front of the round plastic case where they keep slices of pie. Finally a waitress comes over and I'm waiting for her to tell me to move. She doesn't. "What can I get ya?" she says.

"Oh, nothing, I'm just looking at the pies," I say.

I often come to town alone. No one bothers me. No one pays attention to a kid like me. I like that. I'm tall for my age. I'm light skinned and I'm fat. Oh, I can say it because I know I'm fat. Being big helps me move around town without people asking stupid questions like, "Are you lost?" Or "Where's your mother?"

Today I'm going to buy a ten-cent bottle of red nail polish at Kress' and a five-cent bag of peanuts from Mr. Nuts where it always smells like something's burning. I go into the Wolf and Marx Department Store because they have good air conditioning and I make believe it's winter. There's also a perfume counter which makes the store smell sweet. When the sidewalk gets too hot I go into another store.

There are several on Houston Street. I like the fabric store, all they sell is fabric. There must be thousands of bolts of material in every color in the world. I come in one door, make my way through the 'In Season Now' section. I look and I touch and most of all I like the way the store smells. I think of clean clothes. I go out the other door and follow the steps down to the river. It's much cooler here. The sidewalk is at the edge of the water. The river sounds angry, it doesn't like being trapped by cement walls. It rushes along trying to get out of town where it's finally free and can meander at its own pace. I don't stay here too long. It smells like pee. High school boys and girls come here to neck. I don't like to look at them, I feel embarrassed. I don't know why since its not my panties the boys are playing with. Sometimes I see a turtle or tiny fish, but not often.

We can go into the pool on Monday, Wednesday and Friday. The White Only days are Tuesday, Thursday, Saturday and Sunday. Today is Thursday and it's so hot. The sweat is running down my fat cheeks.

I forgot to tell you I hate my name. My name is the sound a hippo makes when it yawns. AOU-ROAR-RAH. It's really Aurora but my teacher can't say it right. I hate roll call when she calls out AOU-ROAR-RAH. The other day a new, young teacher said to me, "I like your name." I made an ugly face and she said to me, "No, really, do you know that it means dawn?" I looked at her and she said, "You know, dawn, the beginning of the day."

Well, I like Dawn. It's a lot better than that awful yawning sound. I'm not telling anyone that my name is Dawn. It's my secret.

I line up with the other kids waiting for the pool to open. The girls are in one line and the boys in another. I don't care if the lady who takes the dime yells at me, I'm going to try to get in. I see the blue water and smell the chlorine. I can't wait. The line moves slowly and when it's almost my turn I start feeling scared but there's no time for fear, besides it's so hot. As long as I don't open my mouth maybe she'll think I'm white. I hand her my two nickels and she gives me a safety pin with the number of the metal basket for my clothes. I quickly take them off. I'm already wearing my bathing suit underneath. The cement between the dressing room and the pool is burning my feet. I walk to the shallow end and very slowly put my feet in the water. Oh, it's cold and it feels so good. I walk in a little further until the cold water touches my butt and I want to giggle. I walk until the water comes to under my chin. Now I'm so light, I don't weigh anything. I'm Dawn, the mermaid, and I glide in the water and I'm going to stay here until my fingers and toes are wrinkled.

I see some kids from my neighborhood. They're all sweaty and hot. They're pressed against the chain link fence that's around the pool.

"Hey, fatty," they call out, "today's not for Mexicans!"

I don't even look at them. I just swim away. Right now I'm not white or Mexican, I'm Dawn the beautiful mermaid and I like it just fine.

The Ladies

"Go straight to church and don't even think about sitting in the front pew."

Every Sunday I'd hear the same thing from my mother.

"Why don't they let someone else sit there," I'd say. "I think those old women in black have been sitting there for a hundred years."

"Yes. And you're not the one that's going to make them move."

With all that said, I walked to church picking up my friends as I went along. Their mothers had also warned them about the front pew.

I don't even know why we boys were made to go to church. We didn't understand most of what was being said. We went because we were told to. The old usher would make us sit where he could keep his eye on us. We stood and we knelt and we crossed ourselves and did whatever the others were doing. Most of the time I spent looking at the statues of the saints that lined the walls. Some were very gory and frightening. Saint Sebastian was tied to a tree and had all these arrows stuck in him and Saint Lucy's eyes were on the plate she was holding in her hands. Going to church was enough to give me nightmares for days.

As I got older I went to church less and less. When I did go I was curious to see if the old women were still in the front pew.

"Mother, what do you know about those old women?" I asked.

"First of all," she replied, "you know that everyone calls them The Ladies, so don't be disrespectful, there's no need for that."

"Alright, now tell me what you know about them."

"They're sisters and no one really knows how old they are. I've seen them since I was a little girl. They've never married. The younger one was courted by a doctor from El Paso and he turned out to be already married to another girl. It broke her heart. Their father owned a small mine and with the money he built the big house near the square. When he died they put on the black and that was almost fifty years ago."

Besides the house they must have had some money because they hired people to do housework and keep the gardens. The house was the biggest and best in our little town. People would bring their out of town friends to see the beautiful house, but only from the outside. The Ladies didn't entertain or invite people to visit. Only the town doctor would call when they needed his services.

One day, my uncle who ran the fruit stand near the plaza, asked me to take a basket of sweet limes to The Ladies. I was afraid. What if they yell at me and throw me off their door step? I mustered up the courage and convinced myself that it was a good test for me to try something that made me uncomfortable. If I do well, I told myself, I'll feel proud.

"Buenas tardes," I called out as I knocked on the heavy wood door. I heard footsteps approaching. The door opened and there stood one of The Ladies. She was the youngest and also the smallest. I had no idea I was so much taller than she. She looked up at me as I handed her the basket.

"My uncle sent these limes for you," I said.

"And they are beautiful. Please thank him for us." She spoke softly and carefully formed each word.

I kept my eyes lowered and focused on my shoeless feet. A boy my age would never look an adult in the eyes, it was considered disrespectful. I controlled my urge to look straight into her face. What color were her eyes? Did she have a nice smile?

"Yes, ma'm. I'll tell him."

I turned to walk away.

"Wait a moment," she said. "I'll be right back."

I tried to look inside the house but the door blocked my view.

"Here," she said. "This is for you."

I extended my hand and she put a coin in it.

"No," I protested. "You don't have to give me anything."

"Of course I do," she said.

This gave me the chance to look at her. Wispy white hair framed her face, she was smiling and her dark eyes sparkled.

Instead of it being a time to pray,

Sunday Mass became the time I spied on The Ladies. There was no malice in what I did. Curiosity was my motivator. I tried to sit close enough to see them but not so close as to cause the old usher to get suspicious.

Each of them carried a prayer book. They knew the responses without even looking at the pages. The three would sing the hymns in high voices and God forbid anyone started coughing or a kid crying, because the older sister would turn around and glare. That was your signal to shut up or get out. They wore black dresses and shiny black shoes with silver buckles. Their heads were covered with black lace shawls that draped across their shoulders. At the end of Mass, most people would remain in their pews until The Ladies walked up the aisle, stopped at the holywater font, blessed themselves and left the church.

This is what they did every Sunday. It appeared that time stood still as far as they were concerned. I never noticed them aging. I could tell my father and mother were getting older, not to mention my grandpa who aged by the day.

Not too long after this, when I turned fourteen, my godfather asked me to move to the town where he lived so that I could start an apprenticeship in his furniture shop. My parents were happy for me to be given such an opportunity. In my heart I would have rather gone to the university but I knew that for a family such as ours it was impossible.

Time passed quickly. Months became years. On one of my visits home I asked my mother, "What ever happened to The Ladies?"

"The only one left is the little one. The one who gave you the coin. Do you remember?"

Five years had passed since that day when I brought them the limes and I remembered it as if it were yesterday.

"Is she still in the big house?" I asked.

"Oh no," answered my mother. "She couldn't live by herself, so the Carmelite Nuns took her to live with them in the convent."

"What about the beautiful house?" I asked.

"Oh, it's such a shame. The house was boarded up and abandoned for a long time. Then a man from Tampico bought it and now it's a rooming house. No one cares for it. It's no longer beautiful. The gardens are neglected and the house looks terrible."

I walked to town. I wanted to see the house for myself. I felt fear anticipating what I would find. My mother was right. The big house was no longer beautiful. I tried to understand my feeling of sadness. It wasn't my house. I was never invited in. Walking home I realized the house and The Ladies were in some inexplicable way tangled up in my memories of childhood. Fantasies of what the inside of the house looked like? What foods were served on their table? What was it like having money? These were things I didn't have, and I realized early I probably never would. Yet, I didn't envy them.

I created stories about them. They were unsuspecting characters in the tales of mystery and intrigue hatched in the head of a child. We were all ordinary people. The Ladies were the only ones I knew that lived life differently than the rest of us.

"Mother, can I visit her?" I asked.

"Who are you talking about?"

"The Lady, the little one that's with the nuns."

"I suppose you can, but why do you want to?"

I couldn't answer the question because I didn't know myself. I just felt I had to do this.

As I walked to the convent I questioned my motives. I still didn't have a good answer. I rang the bell at the convent door and a little window slid open. I couldn't see anyone but the voice of a young woman asked.

"Can I help you?"

The cloistered Carmelites never left the convent once they took their vows. People said their families could visit once a year. The nuns never got to go home again, even when their parents died.

"Good morning, sister. I don't know if I'm allowed, I want to visit..." It hit me like a ton of bricks. What an idiot I was. I didn't know The Lady's name. I had known them my entire life as The Ladies. I felt like a fool. I was ready to turn around and run when the nun's voice came from behind the opening in the door.

"You want to visit the Little Lady, right?"

I answered despite the lump in my throat. "Yes sister, please, can I?"

"Wait here. I'll get Mother Superior."

Mother Superior opened the door. She had a friendly face and that's all I could see because she kept her hands tucked beneath the front panel of her heavy brown habit.

"No one visits anymore. She's very old you know and she remembers very little. She forgets where she is," Mother Superior said. "She may not remember you."

"She may not remember me but I remember her," I said.

I was escorted to a small garden where the Little Lady sat in a rocking chair. She was wrapped in a shawl. She looked so small and fragile. I bent over so she could see my face.

"Do you remember me? I'm the one who brought you the sweet limes. But that was a long time ago."

I took her hand in mine. Her thin fingers, covered with skin so fine and delicate I could see the blue veins beneath it, gently squeezed my hand. She smiled. I sat on a short stool next to her and held her hand as she gently rocked back and forth. She didn't say a word but I hoped she could hear me. I spoke slowly and clearly.

"I remember how you and your sisters sat in the front pew every Sunday. I've been away learning how to make furniture. I'm coming back and I hope to have my own shop. Do you remember the flocks of wild parrots that lived in your avocado trees? They sure were noisy."

I hoped my ramblings made her understand that I remembered and cared.

She just smiled.

I gently kissed her hand and said good-bye.

Two years passed. I moved back to my town where I planned to open my shop. My parents were old and I wanted to be close to them.

"Mother, did the last Little Lady die?" I asked.

"Yes. It wasn't too long after you saw her. The nuns had a nice funeral for her and now all three sisters are buried next to each other."

I felt sad. It wasn't like the sadness I felt when my grandpa died, but still a sense of loss for a time in my life that was gone, just like The Ladies.

"You'll be glad to know," my mother interrupted my thoughts, "the house has a new owner. He's repairing it and they say it will be as beautiful as when The Ladies were alive."

I walked to the plaza. I followed the same streets as when I was a boy and I could still tell you where each of my friends lived.

"Hey Carlos," I yelled out.

"When did you get back?" Carlos responded.

I walked through the plaza and sat on a bench across the street from the house. It was a hive of activity. Shutters were being hung, walls were being painted, gardeners were trimming neglected trees. The house would be beautiful again.

A white haired old man sat next to me. We greeted each other as was the custom.

"Buenos dias Señor," I said.

"What do you think?" he asked. He didn't look at me but motioned with his chin at the house.

"I think it's good that someone is taking care of the house."

"They say it's haunted," he whispered.

"Have you seen anything?" I asked.

"No. I haven't, but some say they have. They say the spirits of The Ladies who lived here many years ago are still in the house."

"No sir," I said. I didn't hide the smile on my face. "No need to worry about that. I'm certain The Ladies have far better things to do and if they were going to haunt anywhere, it would be the front pew."

Jimmy

I thought all white people were rich. I knew all Mexicans were poor. Then in fifth grade a white boy named Jimmy came into my class. I couldn't figure out why he'd want to be with us when he could be with rich people. But he wasn't rich. He was just as poor as we were. He was the nicest boy in school. He was hit by a car and killed on Highway 90 as he walked home from school one day. I wish I'd known him better. I've never forgotten him.

The One-Eyed Saint
of Muddy Creek

After a night of drunkenness and debauchery the man was walking home. In order to get there he needed to cross the creek which was usually dry. This night however, a torrential downpour had swollen the creek with fast running brown water.

He walked along the bank looking for a place to cross. The water was deeper and stronger than he anticipated. The water swirled around him. He lost his balance and within seconds he was swept away, arms flailing, legs kicking. He desperately tried to keep his head above water.

"Oh God!" he cried out. "Please don't let me drown. My poor wife and children need me. Help!"

On the bank of the creek stood a stranger. When he heard the man yelling for help he picked up a log and threw it into the water. The drowning man grabbed the floating piece of wood and the current brought him to the edge. The stranger helped the man out of the creek.

"Thank you, oh, thank you sir," tears running down his face. "If you hadn't come along I surely would have drowned. You saved my life."

The stranger, tall, dark, wore his hair long, was dressed in old clothes and most definitely had only one eye, having lost the other in a barroom brawl two years earlier.

While the wet, but now sober man caught his breath, the stranger disappeared into the thicket. The man looked all around and when he couldn't find him exclaimed in a loud voice, "Thank you, God. You sent your holy saint to save me. I promise to show you my gratitude for this miracle."

He walked home carrying the log that had saved his life. He thought for a long time. How could he show his gratitude?

"I could make a cross, but there are so many of them in the church already. I could never carve a Madonna as beautiful as the one we already have. I know!" he exclaimed, "I will carve a statue of the One-Eyed Santo who saved me."

After working in the fields all day he came home to his wife and children. He stopped drinking and became a devoted husband and father.

Wanting to remain anonymous, he carved at night when everyone was sleeping. He sat outside and worked on the log by the light of a single candle.

When the statue was done, he wrapped it in burlap and in the middle of the night, walked to the creek. He attached it to the stump of a tree. This was the perfect place where everyone would see it.

He knelt down before it. "Thank you again for saving my life. I hope you like your statue. You and God now know that I kept my promise."

By the next morning people were talking about the statue.

"I think it's a miracle," said the baker.

"I think it's the devil," said the butcher.

"I think whoever carved it wasn't very good," said the goat herder.

"I think it's good and we should keep it," said the candy vendor.

Even though the town boasted electric lights and one telephone, no one understood how either one worked or where they came from. It was all a mystery. So the appearance of the Saint was only one more thing to accept and not question.

The first sign of acceptance was a small bunch of wildflowers in a rusted tin can. Later someone left a small candle stuck to a flat rock.

People started coming to the statue of the Saint to ask for favors and intercession.

"Dear One-Eyed Saint, you who can see better with one eye than me with two, please help me decide should I marry the mailman or the butcher's son?" The pretty girl bowed her head and clasped her hands in reverence.

Farmers came for help, too. "Please guide me Holy Saint, should I plant corn or alfalfa?"

They were convinced the answers to their prayers and questions came from a heavenly source when in reality they already knew what it was they needed or wanted to do. If it turned out poorly they could blame the Saint and no one would think any less of them for making a bad choice.

In a short time the tree stump that held the statue was surrounded by flowers, candles and thank you notes.

36

People came from nearby towns and villages to see and pray to the miraculous statue. Entire families spent their Sunday afternoon sitting along the creek. Children played in the trickle of water and women argued about who needed a miracle first.

"It's a sacrilege!" said the mayor. "Our very own dear Saint has to sit outside in the rain and cold. He should have a place in the church."

A committee made up of the town's important people demanded that the priest let them bring the Saint indoors.

The priest, an already unpopular fellow, acquiesced to the demands and a corner was designated for the One-Eyed Saint of Muddy Creek.

"I will build a beautiful pedestal," said the carpenter. "Our Saint deserves the best."

It wasn't long before all sorts of testaments to the Saint's amazing power covered the pedestal. An entire rack of votive candles was set up and a place to hold the numerous flower arrangements that arrived daily. Pinned to the wall were pictures of men, women, children, horses and other farm animals that had been cured. Sons who passed school exams and lonely hearts who found love, all thanks to the statue . The non-believers claimed he was credited with far more miracles than he had actually performed.

And so it was. The people loved their very own Saint so much that they came up with a special feast day when every person in the town put a patch over their left eye in his honor.

In the meantime, the tall stranger with the one eye moved to Mexico City where he found a doctor who fitted him with a glass eye prosthesis. It was a perfect match. Feeling quite confident about his good looks, he had a haircut and a shave, bought new clothes and spent the next six months visiting every brothel in the city. He later married a pretty woman, fathered ten children and never, ever, knew he was the One-Eyed Saint of Muddy Creek.

Amen.

The Green Dress

In the central valley of California, raisins are dried in the sun. The clusters of grapes are laid on paper squares at the base of the vine. Though no longer attached to the vine, they remain close to their life source. They are purposely abandoned for many days. Their time in the sun turns them dark and wrinkled and they become sweeter.

Two women sit side by side in the bright sunlight. They remind me of raisins. Their faces dark and wrinkled. They sit for a long time without saying a word, something only old friends can do.

The woman in the green dress turns to her companion, "I dreamed of Joe last night."

With a wide grin and a chuckle the other woman says, "I also dream about the boys I knew, sometimes we dance."

They both start laughing and the woman in the green dress reaches over and takes her friend's hand.

They keep laughing.

Someone Should Change the Sign

Regardless of who we are or where we come from, we're all in the same boat. The lady doctor talks to us about having our babies, most of it we can't understand and in the end all we want to know is how much will it hurt.

She smiles and says, "Some of you could have an easy delivery." She doesn't say anything about the girls that labor for days.

"I ain't gonna give my baby away," Loud Girl announces to all within earshot.

"So what are you gonna do?" asks Big Red Haired Girl.

"I'm takin' my baby and we're going to

41

Dallas, I'll get a job, I'll do anything."

Bird Girl won't look anyone in the eye, keeps to herself and hardly says a word.

I call her Bird Girl because she's tiny, in spite of her belly, and always looks afraid.

"Eat your food," I tell her. "Your baby needs it."

She just pushes it around her plate so that the potatoes wind up where the carrots used to be and hardly eats a thing. I can see how some of us got in trouble. I think some here went and looked for it, but not her. She had to really be in love. I bet it was a Bird Boy.

The small, neat sign near the entrance reads, "HOME FOR UNWED MOTHERS." The truth is this isn't home and we're not mothers. We're girls who did something in the back seat of a borrowed car or on the ground in the woods that can never be changed. It will stay with us till we die. I think the sign should say, "HOME FOR GIRLS WITH REGRETS."

Some girls get mail. I don't. No one writes to Fat Girl with Swollen Feet. No one writes, "We miss you," or, "Can't wait to see you." The counselor wants to see me.

"Your aunt called," she says. "She didn't want to speak with you, she wants me to tell you and have you understand, you can't go home with the baby." I don't say a word but move my head up and down so she knows I hear what she's telling me. She's telling me I must give it up. I won't let myself think about this, not yet.

Bird Girl has gone into labor. We're not allowed anywhere near the delivery room. We hear she had a rough time. The next day we learn her baby was born dead. We register the shock in different ways. None of us have ever thought our babies could die.

A man carries a small suitcase and a woman walks with her arm around Bird Girl's shoulders. A car is waiting. Bird Girl never looks back. I wave from the window. I know she can't see me.

Winter comes hard. I look out the window and the sky is grey, the color of steel. The trees are bare and I don't see any birds. I press my cheek against the window and it feels like ice. I can't get warm no matter what I do. My belly gets bigger each day.

Loud Girl turned eighteen a week before her baby came. As soon as she could she bundled up her baby boy and left.

My heartburn is so bad now that at night I sleep sitting up in my bed with my face leaning on the wall. The pain wakes me up. I feel deep hard cramps in my lower belly. I feel wet and warm between my legs, I'm afraid to look. I'm shaking. A nurse brings a wheelchair and now the wet is pouring out of me and I can't stop it. I'm taken to a room with a hospital bed, a big clock on the wall and a metal waste basket. The pain goes up and down. Each time it comes back harder. I'm all alone and I'm scared.

A nurse comes in and says, "Spread your legs." She doesn't speak to me but under her breath I hear her say, "This one's ready." I'm in pain and I'm confused and I want to yell out, "No, no, I'm not ready." But there's no stopping this no matter how much I want it to.

The doctor and nurse go about their duties, they never talk to me. They seem to ignore me and when I cry out in pain no one says, "There, there, it'll be over soon." I push when told to, big hot tears run down my face and I feel the baby coming out. I hear the baby cry and the doctor says, "It's a girl." He's not talking to me.

The baby is wrapped up and taken to the nursery. I wake up hours later. The belly is gone. There's a thick pad between my legs and when I move it hurts down there.

The counselor comes in holding a bunch of papers and asks, "Have you decided?" As if I have a choice. I feel my mouth moving and I hear my voice saying, "Yes, I don't want her."

"Do you want to see her?" she asks.

"No, I can't."

I walk down the same walkway as Bird Girl, I don't look back either. The car takes me to the bus station. I have a ticket and some money for food. I sit alone near the door. No one notices me. No one knows my heart is broken. The voice on the speaker announces, "last bus for San Antonio boarding now."

Black Moon Rising

Was the old man telling the truth? Did he really know these things? These terrible frightening things.

"They gather and fly. They make their way to a meeting place. There are so many of them that it would scare a man to death just to look at them," he said.

"Do they really use sticks to fly on?" I asked.

"Ha-ha," the old man mocked, "that's a child's tale. I'm talking about real witches, the evil ones that have traded their souls to the devil in order to have all the power. They fly at night, when there's no moon, they turn themselves into black birds. Horrible birds with beaks as sharp as knives."

"But what do they want? Why are they flying over our village? We have nothing."

"Oh yes we do," he said. "We have souls. They have lost theirs and will do anything to get one. Do you remember a while back when they found that man in the corn field?"

"Yes," I answered. "He was always drunk. I heard he fell in the dark and hit his head on a rock and that's how he died."

The old man didn't look at me but asked, "Did you also know that when they found him his eyes had been pecked out?" No, I didn't know that and just the thought made me shiver.

"What can we do?" I pleaded.

"Stay in your house. Lock your windows and doors and don't come out, no matter what you hear. If you think you hear your brother's voice calling you, don't go, it's a trick." Could the old man be lying to me? Why would he?

I finished my chores and made sure I was home well before dark. My mother wanted to know why I was so quiet. I didn't answer. I shared a small room with my brother and sister. We each had a small cot, and a mattress stuffed with dried corn husks. Even my slightest movement made a sound like the rustling of dead leaves under my feet.

Mother came into the room to bless us

and say good night. She made the sign of the cross on our foreheads. Tonight I wanted more blessings. I rummaged through the wooden box, where I kept my belongings, until I found the rosary given to me by the nuns. Mother turned down the oil lamp. Slowly the flame became smaller and smaller until the room was dark.

It wasn't long before I heard my brother snoring and my sister's soft breathing. I shut my eyes but I wasn't going to sleep tonight. I was going to wait and listen for the black birds that were foretold by the old man. I wandered in and out of sleep. Then I started to hear strange sounds. Eerie high pitched bird screams. First there was one, then others. I could hear the flapping of their wings as they flew over our house. All of a sudden the breath was sucked out of me when I heard something on the thatched roof. I could hear a bird scratching the dried fronds. It hopped around from place to place. I held my rosary tight against my heart. I shut my eyes and pulled the blankets and pillow over my head. I don't know how much time passed but when I pushed my head out from beneath the blankets, the terrible sounds had stopped. I looked around the darkened room and the only sound I heard was my brother who continued to snore. At some point I must have fallen asleep because when I woke up it was morning.

My mother was at the wood stove cooking and we were dressing when someone came running down the road screaming and yelling. People ran toward the creek.

"There's a body down by the creek!" the man yelled. My brother ran out the door and followed the others. When he returned, he told us, "It's a woman. She's dead. No one knows who she is." What about her eyes? I wanted to know, but was too afraid to ask. Could anyone tell by looking at her that her soul had been taken?

I wrapped a piece of bread and some cheese in a cloth and ran to the old man's house. He was already sitting outside. I handed him the food and sat down next to him.

"Did you hear them?" I asked.

"Yes, even in the pitch black of night I could see them."

"Do you think they killed the woman found near the creek?" The old man didn't answer. He patted my head, got up from his chair, took the bundle and went inside his house.

I ran home, I was late and my family was already working in the corn field. That night I asked my brother, "Do you know about the black birds that flew over the village last night? Someone told me they are evil and can steal your soul."

My brother looked at me. "What are you saying? Did the old man tell you this?" he asked. " I hope you don't believe it."

"The old man told me witches turn themselves into black birds and look for souls to replace the ones they sold to the devil," I said.

He placed his hands firmly on my shoulders. "Listen, what you saw was the birds going back to where they come from. All birds do it. They travel in flocks and it's a natural thing. There's nothing mysterious or evil about it."

"What about the dead woman?" I asked.

"It had nothing to do with the birds," he said.

That night I rested easier. I wasn't bothered when Mother put out the oil lamp. I was falling asleep when I heard scratching on the roof. I sat straight up in bed. My eyes were wide open but I couldn't see because it was so dark. In my panic all I could think was that the evil bird, with it's sharp beak, would work its way into my room. I never felt fear like this before.

All of a sudden a hand grabbed my arm. I wanted to scream but the fear was so great I couldn't utter a sound. I think I was about to faint when I heard my brother's voice.

"It's only a night bird trying to catch a mouse on the roof," he said. "Don't be afraid. There are no witches."

"But the old man..."

My brother interrupted. "The old man is lonely. He likes that you visit him. He tells you tales to keep you coming back. Maybe you shouldn't believe everything he says."

"Maybe you're right," I said, "but I'm still scared." My brother pushed his cot next to mine and held my hand for a long time. "Please don't tell anyone how frightened I was," I whispered.

"Don't worry, I won't."

Maybe You're a Gypsy Too

It was our second day in this small Irish village and as I turned a corner I saw a Gypsy caravan. Not entirely unusual since many Roma still live in this part of the country. My brain was flooded with images of Marlene Dietrich in the old movie *Golden Earrings*. I have seen the film many times and know the ending. The beautiful Gypsy girl saves the British officer. They fall in love but, alas, they must part.

I approached the old horse and greeted him in a soft voice. He let me pat his neck. I walked around the caravan admiring the colors of the numerous coats of paint it had received over the years. The wheels were car tires and they looked like they'd been up and down many roads. As I came to the back of the caravan, the door was flung open and there stood a man.

"Don't let me frighten you, girl."

"Oh no, you didn't frighten me, you just surprised me."

I appreciated his calling me "girl" since we both looked to be near seventy.

"I love your - - your," I stammered. I didn't know the correct word to use. Was it a caravan or vehicle? Was the word caravan used by Gypsies in Ireland and was the word Gypsy an acceptable word?

"You mean my home." He jumped to the pavement and I followed him. He climbed onto the seat and took the reins in his hands. He smiled at me and extended his hand.

"Come on girl, let me take you for a ride."

I couldn't let this opportunity pass me by. I took his hand and he pulled me to the seat next to him. The horse knew where to go and as we rounded the corner there stood my husband and our friends, the looks on their faces ranged from surprise to horror. I waved to them as we trotted down the road. Green hills on one side and blue ocean on the other. I extended my hand and said, "My name is Kate, thank you for inviting me."

I wanted to ask so many questions but I didn't want to be rude. I finally got the nerve. "What is the correct name, or what do you prefer to be called?" Immediately I knew it sounded stupid. I hesitated, "I mean, where are you from, originally?" This sounded worse than the first. He laughed and said, "I was born in Ireland, so I'm Irish." He knew what I wanted to know and he continued.

"Some people call us Gypsies and others refer to us as Roma, but the one word that describes me best is Traveler."

"Thank you for sharing this with me, I feel we're friends now."

He smiled, "I'm glad, we all need friends."

"Come on you old horse, those cars behind us will start tooting their horns if you don't hurry."

I smiled and waved to the cars as they passed us on the road. Some people would smile, others just stared. I hoped they believed we were a couple of old Travelers on our way to the Camargue to celebrate the Feast of the Gypsy Saints.

"I think I'm Gypsy too." The words tumbled out of my mouth before I could stop them.

"Why so, Kate? Where did your parents

come from?"

I realized it was very improbable that my parents were Gypsies. "My parents were born in Mexico, I was born in Texas," I answered him with disappointment in my voice.

He looked pensive as he maneuvered his horse to a side road. "Well now, you know Travelers are in all parts of the world, even Mexico," he said.

We returned to the spot where we met. I took his hand, "Thank you so much. You have no idea what this means to me. I won't forget." Our parting was brief and sincere. As I walked away I turned to wave one last time.

"I think you're right girl," he shouted to me. "I think you're Gypsy, too."

I stayed up to watch *Golden Earrings* tonight. It's still as wonderful and romantic as I remember. Only this time it has special meaning. I'm thinking of my friend in his caravan and I wonder where he is tonight.

The Cat in the Window

The old man takes the picture from the shelf, wipes it with the sleeve of his shirt and hands it to me.

"This is Pearl. I loved her and she loved me. She loved to dance. My wife would say, 'get away from that window, people will think you're crazy dancing with that cat.'

I found Pearl, or she found me, down by the railroad tracks. I used to take a short cut home and I was walking by the tracks when I heard a weak, little cry from some tall grass, I looked and there she was. Frightened and hungry but most of all very lonely. I put her inside my jacket and brought her home. For a long time she cowered in the corner. She came out when she felt safe. I'd carry her in my arms and that's how the dancing got started. She grew into a beautiful cat. She'd sit on the window sill and look out. There were times when I could see the sadness in her eyes. Almost like she remembered what she'd been through."

Maids

It is well after sundown, when the dinner dishes have been washed and put away, that you see them walking to the bus stop. Hunched-over women wearing ill fitting uniforms. They carry brown paper bags in which there might be a sweater and a coin purse, perhaps a blouse or something the Lady doesn't want.

These women with beautiful names like, Guadalupe, are now answering to children who call them "Loo-Pay." Maria is now "Mary," and Consuelo is shortened to "Connie."

They carry a rosary in their pocket and pray a Hail Mary during the spin cycle. If they are daring, they switch the radio to Mexican music, being quick to change it back when they hear the car drive in.

Blessed Benny the Benevolent

Maybe it was named for MARvelous and FAbulous. M-A-R-F-A. Marfa, Texas. I'd never heard of it and I'm sure I'm not alone. The good looking truck driver with the million dollar smile promised to take me all the way to L.A. We pulled into a truck stop.

"Let's get some coffee," he said. I grabbed my backpack and he took my suitcase.

"Hey, what's up?" I asked.

"Let's go inside, I'll tell you there. The company's checking between El Paso and L.A. and if I get caught with you in the truck that'll be it for me." He looked sorry he had to dump me.

"Take care Chula," he said as he handed me a twenty and my suitcase.

I didn't move or look at him. I suppose I should be thankful he didn't kick me out in the middle of the desert. It was still dark, hours before sunrise; it was already hot. I walked a couple of blocks and realized how useless it was since it was still dark. I came back to the truck stop, paid for a cup of stale coffee and asked the fat guy behind the counter if I could hang out for a while. He grunted. I took that as a yes. I sat on the broken picnic table near the restrooms and watched the sun come up. Marfa looked better in the dark. It was far from marvelous and fabulous. I needed to think fast. I had no job or place to stay, and even in this podunk town the little money I had wouldn't last long. I cleaned up in the truck stop restroom and walked into town. I just needed to make enough money to get to L.A. I stopped at every place on the two block stretch of the main street.

"Do you need any help?"

"No, not today."

"Could you use another waitress?"

"Nah, business ain't too good."

And so it went. The laundry, the 7-11, the liquor store. It looked like no one was hiring.

Divine Providence must have had a soft spot in its heart for me. I turned on a side street lined with drab houses and there in the middle of the block was a bright green house with a sign in the window. WANTED: DOG GROOMER.

I put on my most sincere smile and walked in. The bell hanging from the screen door announced my entry. A person came out from the back carrying two tiny dogs. One in each arm. I couldn't tell if it was a man or a woman. The clothing didn't help. It was an explosion of fabrics and colors, a mix of Hawaiian and Cinco de Mayo.

The voice was definitely masculine. The smile could have been either. He looked around in an exaggerated manner as though he was looking for something on the floor.

"So where's the doggie?" he asked.

"Oh no, I don't have a dog. I want to ask about the job." He looked at me hard.

"Do you have experience? Where have you groomed before? Do you know dogs?" He bombarded me with questions.

I heard myself saying, "I love dogs - I grew up with dogs."

The corner of his mouth crinkled up and he started laughing. "Do you want to explain that, are you talking about your pets or your family?"

His face melted with laughter at his own joke. The little dogs bounced up and down in his chubby arms. He handed me the two tiny dogs and reached into his smock for a colored bandana to wipe the tears from his eyes and the sweat from his face.

"You're not from around here?"

"No, I'm not. I need work real bad and I'm willing to work hard," I said.

He retrieved the dogs from me and pressed them to his chest. He walked around me like he was sizing me up.

"Look," he said, "I don't want to be a shit about it, but you look a little dented here and there, what's your story?"

My polite smile dissolved. "I'm thirty-seven, I'm going to L.A., my sister's there. I think I can find a job or at least have a place to stay while I look. A trucker with a killer smile said he'd take me there then changed his mind and here I am."

He didn't speak but motioned me to follow. He put the little dogs in a pen. He pointed to a stool and I sat on it. He pulled the turban off his perfectly round and bald head, filled two cups with coffee and handed me one.

"So what's the rest of the story?" he asked.

I sipped slowly before answering personal questions from someone I'd just met. At this point I had nothing to lose. "My life was nothing and going nowhere. My last boyfriend left me for a younger woman, he told me I was starting to remind him of his mother."

This man, who looked like a parade float, reached toward me, gently placed one finger on my hand. I hadn't noticed his eyes. They were the bluest I'd ever seen. "Oh life," he said, "she can be cruel. My motto is damn the torpedos and full steam ahead."

What the hell was he talking about, torpedos and steam! I interrupted him, "I worked in a bakery for years. I'm a good worker. I have lots of experience. I learn fast."

"Listen," he said, "I pay by the hour. Sometimes, and I mean almost never, you get tips. I need help with the bigger dogs. Bathing, brushing, cleaning cages and all sorts of other sophisticated and exciting chores like picking up poop and mopping floors."

"What's the pay?" I asked

"I can do six an hour and you can stay in the room upstairs. No one uses it anymore."

I would have been beyond crazy not to take it. "That sounds great, can I start today, now?"

"Sure, but perhaps we need to know each other's names."

Benny was willing to teach me and I wanted to do right. This rotund, bald, walking thrift shop rack was my knight in shining armor. The first day melted into the second and so on and so on and at last count I had been at Benny Beauties six months.

I learned Benny had opened his door and his heart to others before me. Some younger, some older. All lost, and his kindness helped us find our way.

Benny and I worked well together. We settled into a routine. I answered the phone, which seldom rang, but which he refused to answer. I walked and fed the dogs and kept the place clean. In the small kennel he kept two old dogs. "They're brothers, you know, they have always been together." When their owner died of old age, Benny took them in. He and the dogs kept each other company and Benny spent hours talking to the dogs.

"Well, if you ask me I think this is a ridiculous situation and I for one wouldn't put up with it for one minute!" I hurried in to see who Benny was talking to and it was the dogs. They were sitting, side by side, very still, listening intently to Benny's tirade. The confused look on my face must have said it all. Benny smiled and winked at me.

Marfa, Texas seemed to attract a peculiar type. This tiny town of less than two thousand, smack in the middle of the Chihuahuan Desert, has been around since 1883. Even then, it had its share of seekers and dreamers, loners and misfits. People left you alone. They didn't want to tell you their story and didn't want to hear yours.

Marfa's claim to fame came in 1955 when the movie *Giant* was shot here. The other reason people come is to see the mysterious lights that appear in the desert. The Marfa Lights, as they are called, have been reported since the 1800s. What a hoax, I thought. Locals swear these mysterious lights exist and it's such a big deal the town built a viewing station nine miles out on highway 67 near the old Air Force base. The few tourists that come through Marfa can't pass up the opportunity of seeing these mystical lights for themselves. I heard the stories, which I didn't believe, just a myth, I thought.

Benny and I secretly hoped the mysterious lights did exist and that we would see them some night. He'd put blankets on the back seat and load up the old dogs. We'd pick up a couple of beers and head out to the viewing station. We came often and all we ever saw were jackrabbits and tourists. Sometimes we talked, sometimes we just sat there quietly looking at the desert and listening to the dogs snore. When we talked, Benny called this our accounting class. He'd say, "We're accounting for our lives." One night he shared more than usual.

"I didn't always live here, you know. I was a cute tight-assed city boy. Paul, the apple of my eye, the man on whom the sun rose and set, got cancer. I took such good care of him, I never left his side. Then on a starlit night, the love of my life died in my arms. I wanted to die too. I quit my job, sold everything and started driving East and this is as far as I got."

Benny and I told each other many things. Things no one else knew. At the end, Benny would say, "You see, it wasn't all bullshit. There's a reason for everything."

Time passed quickly. The relentless summer heat was replaced by a welcomed fall. The desert trees changed their color and the evenings were surprisingly cold. I knew the day was coming when it would be time for me to leave.

"Benny," I said, "I think I'll be leaving in a couple of weeks."

He smiled. "You mustn't miss your appointment with destiny." Something only Benny could say. I took his hand.

"You know you saved my life? How do I thank you?"

"Don't think about it kiddo, just live well," was his reply.

The day before I was to leave Benny said, "Let's give those god-dammed lights another try, what do you say?"

We put sweaters on the dogs and headed out of town. The usual diehards were already there. Some with binoculars, others with cameras. We were there out of habit, not that we expected to see anything. All of a sudden we heard a commotion from the people on the viewing platform. We jumped out of the car to have a better look and we both started shouting. "There! There! Do you see them?" Balls of light were floating just above the desert floor. Others were bouncing up and down. Little ones and big ones. Some seemed to break apart into smaller ones. They were the most beautiful thing I'd ever seen.

The Marfa Lights had proved me wrong. It wasn't a myth, they were real. The lights I didn't believe existed made their presence known. In my head I kept hearing myself saying, "Just because you can't see it, it doesn't mean it's not there." Perhaps it wasn't an accident that I came to this place at this time in my life. I want to believe my lesson was happiness and love are there but I must wait until the time is right.

Early the next morning, Benny drove me to the Greyhound stop. The old dogs and the tiny ones came along. I got my suitcase and walked around to the driver's side. We didn't need to speak. It had all been said. I kissed him on the cheek. Benny took the little dog's paw and moved it up and down like it was waving good-bye, and in a tiny voice he said,

"Bye-bye Miss Poo Poo Caca, I'll miss you."

Torquemada's Slipper
or
La Chancla

Nowadays, most parents don't spank their children and I suppose that's good. In years past, mothers and grandmothers, in a moment of sheer desperation, would fling footwear at misbehaving kids. It was, I imagine, a way to discipline the child without the guilt since it was something other than the hand inflicting pain.

This practice of flying footwear may have been universal but nowhere was it more feared than in the Mexican home. Its mere mention stopped kids in their tracks. It could make the biggest and meanest kid cry, "Please! I'll never do it again." But begging and pleading didn't stop the dreaded "CHANCLA."

71

In non-Mexican homes, when slippers were thrown at children, they were usually the soft, padded, pastel-colored satin ones. In a Mexican home, being hit by a chancla was tantamount to receiving an oncoming SCUD. These so-called "slippers" were made of such items as discarded truck radials, heavy weight leather straps and buckles made from melted down oil derricks.

It was amazing the speed that a flying chancla could reach, even when thrown by an elderly woman. The action of throwing was usually accompanied by the magical incantation, "muchacho maldito" (cursed child), which insured that even if you ducked behind furniture the dreaded chancla would find its target.

On my last visit to Tijuana I watched with interest as people my age, both men and women, pointed to displays in shop windows and store shelves.

"Do you remember how much it hurt?" a man asked his friend.

"My grandma could fling one from the back porch to the end of the yard!"

"Man, she had a good arm."

Chancla = Spanish for slipper

Love Me Tender

I swivel my hips and the women scream. I shake my leg and I hear more screams. I slowly undo the button on my shirt and the girls go crazy.

"More, more," they yell.

I look at them and curl my lip in a perfect Elvis imitation and I snarl into the mic.

"Behave now, baby."

I scan the audience of full-bosomed young women. I focus on one. I sing to her. She screams and feigns fainting. I love it when they scream. My five-piece band is good and we work well together. We always have a gig and the money is good. The marquee reads,

"The Best Elvis Impersonator on The Strip."
"This is must see entertainment!" read the
June, 1970 review in the Las Vegas Sun
News.

I'm looking at myself in the mirror and
the sequined costume doesn't look as sexy
as it did before. My butt has shrunk and my
belly is accentuated by the wide metallic belt.
My dyed black hair is thinning and my scalp
shows.

"Hey, El Vis." That's how he pronounces
Elvis. "Where are you working these days?"

"I'm over at the Chi-Chi Club."

"Oh, you mean the strip joint on 2nd
Avenue?"

"Yep, that's the one."

"I went in one night and all the broads
are old and ugly."

"What do you expect?" I tell him, "when
beer is fifty-cents a glass."

The band left a long time ago. I use a
tape machine that plays the music as I sing. My
audience tonight is two drunks, the bartender
and an old lady with dyed red hair. She glances
at me when I start my set but quickly loses
interest and focuses on her fifty-cent beer. I
change my clothes in the back room.

You can't call it a dressing room because there is none. The strippers and I change behind stacked beer boxes.

"Joe, are you back there?"

"Yea, Frankie, I'll be right out."

"Listen pal, I can't use you anymore. I'm having to let some of the girls go, too. Business has been awful these last few months."

Frankie is a straight guy and I know he's honest.

"Have you tried some of the places over in Henderson?" he asks.

"No, my car couldn't get me to the end of the Strip."

"I have your money and you're always welcome to come in for a beer."

I carefully button and zip my costume. I put it on a hanger and return it to its heavy plastic garment bag.

Tonight I take all my Elvis outfits out of the closet and lay them on the bed. The jumpsuits, the capes, the belts and the scarves, not to mention the shoes studded with rhinestones. The next morning I walk into a place that rents costumes.

"Hi there. You think you might be interested in these?"

"Whatcha got there, buddy?" asks the man behind the counter. "Where in the world did you get these?" He sounds excited.

"They're mine. I'm, or rather, I was in show business."

"Were you an Elvis impersonator?"

"Yep, that's me. I used to be but not anymore."

"My customers will go nuts when they see this stuff. How much do you want?"

"As much as you're willing to pay."

He reaches for his wallet and offers me six one hundred dollar bills. It's more money than I've seen in a long time.

I drive back to my apartment. I live on a short ugly street. There are no trees or grass. My building was built in the 60's and hasn't seen a coat of paint since. This is a part of Las Vegas tourists never see. The only saving grace is that the rent is cheap and the manager isn't a pain in the ass. As soon as I get inside I turn on the old window air conditioner. It struggles to get started. It huffs and puffs and finally a whisper of cold air comes out.

In the old days I would've sat down

with a cold beer and a cigarette. Not anymore. Doctor's orders. I don't want to end up babbling and in diapers at the Desert View Retirement Home. I go there to visit my old neighbor after his stroke. It's not a pretty place.

I have a brother. I think he lives in Utah, I don't know. We lost touch. I thought about settling down but it never happened. There were plenty of women in my life but nothing permanent.

My Social Security check is not enough. It covers the rent and a few other things, but that's it. I need to find a job.

This morning I make a decision. I walk to Mel's barber shop.

"Hey buddy, how's it goin'?" Mel's always cheerful. "It's not time for another dye job."

"I want you to cut it off. I don't want it black anymore," I tell him.

"You mean you want it to go grey?"

"Grey or white, it doesn't matter. The sooner the better."

Mel starts with scissors and finishes with clippers. I look in the mirror and hold in a gasp. I'm an old man.

Every day I check in with the Musician's Union.

"Sorry Joe, nothing's come in today. I'll get a hold of you if any gigs get posted."

It's always the same. No jobs. The guy at the union hall doesn't have the heart to tell me I'm too old. I stop going when the pained look on his face is too much for me.

The senior center gives free lunch. I make sure I get there after the rush. There's nothing more depressing than a bunch of old people in walkers pushing each other out of the way. Mary, a server, usually sits with me when she's done on the line.

"I like your new look. I can see white hair sprouting all over the place," she says.

"I wonder what I'll look like?" I respond.

"What do you mean?"

"I've always had black hair. I've dyed it for years. Hey, maybe the chemicals leaked into my brain? Can I use that as my excuse?"

"Hell no," she says. "If that was the case, ninety-five percent of all the women in Las Vegas could claim insanity."

We both laugh.

"I think you'll look good when your white hair grows out." She runs her cool hand over my bald pate as she walks away.

I read all the want ads in the paper and go to the employment office. There are plenty of jobs in Vegas if you want to work construction or food service. I'm too old for both.   I can't stop looking.   I know there's something out there for me, I just have to find it.

Mel's the one who tells me about an opening he hears of.   I call.

"You're welcome to come in and fill out an application,"   says the woman's voice on the phone.

The thought of sitting in front of someone asking for a job scares me. This is a whole different story than the music gigs I've done for years.

I make sure I look good.   I brush my teeth twice, I check for nose hairs, my nails are trimmed and clean. I put on a white shirt and black pants. This is as good as I'm going to look.

"Hello," I say to the woman at the desk. "I called yesterday and was told to come in."

"Have you worked in retail before?"

"No, but I'm a people person and I learn quickly."

"Have you ever been arrested?"

"No, I have a clean record."

She hands me an application and a pen.

"Can you fill this out now? You can do it in the staff lounge. When you're done bring it back to me."

I go to the staff lounge with its green tinged fluorescent lights, folding tables and hard plastic chairs. Along the walls are soda and snack machines and posters about safety in the workplace. Music is piped in and an old Tony Bennett song comes on. I tilt my head to hear better. A couple of workers, younger than me by at least fifty years, ignore the mellow voice coming from the speaker.

"He can sure sing a ballad."

Neither respond. They're busy with their cell phones.

Today is the first day of my new job. I have never done anything like this before but it can't be that hard. I check in fifteen minutes before my shift and the pretty girl in the office hands me a name tag, a time card and a red vest to wear over my white shirt. Last week I came in for orientation and one hour of training. I think I know what to do.

I walk through the store. It's a big

place. There's lots of shoppers. I thought people would stare at me but no one pays attention. I see other people in red vests. They're restocking shelves or checking prices. They don't look at me either.

I walk to my assigned post. Mothers with kids are coming in. They're trying to keep the kids together. I don't say anything. I'm not sure where or when to start. I see two women. Older women with grey hair. They're wearing pedal pushers and running shoes. They look friendly. If I'm going to start this gig it has to be now and they're my chosen ones.

When they're close enough to hear me I hold an imaginary mic to my mouth, I put my leg out and in my very best Elvis imitation, I curl my lip.

"Welcome to Walmart, baby!"

The Bench

The old men, reminiscent of rusted tin cans, sit on the makeshift bench. They talk of women they loved and women who loved them. Their eyes take on a shine and for a moment you can see the young bucks they used to be. Their ancient eyes, connected to their hearts, tell stories of desire, passion and love.

My Short Career As a Witch

At the age of ten I became a witch. Although ours was a Catholic home, filled with religious statues, and pictures of Jesus, conversations about witches, ghosts and evil spells were common.

"A jealous woman put a curse on her," my mother would say.

People traveled far to find super curse-busters to remove evil spells that brought them bad luck, illness and even death.

"That girl is mean to me," complained my friend Rosie. "I wish she'd go to another school."

Wanting to help my friend in distress I conjured up a curse that guaranteed to stop the bullying.

"Rosie," I said, "write the girl's name on this piece of paper, spear it with this stick. Now, I want you to say the three most awful curse words you know, then spit on it."

We walked around the neighborhood looking for fresh dog poop. The paper bearing the bully's name, having been properly cursed and spat upon was pushed into the poop. It wasn't long that the mean girl and her family moved to Del Rio.

I briefly dabbled in fortune telling and palm reading, but that soon became boring and anyway Rosie's dad brought home a second-hand TV which proved to be much more fun.

Hey, Ugly

Janie and I sit crossed legged in front of her TV. People are talking about the Vietnam War.

"You're either for it or not," Janie says.

"Of course I want the U.S. to win the war, I just don't want my brother to get killed," I tell her.

I want to understand what our soldiers are doing there. I find it hard to concentrate and as soon as I see dead soldiers my brain shuts down. What if that's Leo? My wonderful, goofy brother, a soldier, fighting in the jungle.

"He's serving his country," my dad says.

"We should've stayed in Mexico," I answer.

"This is our country now, and remember, he's not the only boy fighting."

My sweet, gentle brother. The one who yells for me to get the spider out of the tub. The one that always has a piece of chewing gum for me.

In Spanish, my mom asks, "Where is Vietnam? Son Chinos?"

"No Mom," I say. "They're not Chinese, they're Vietnamese."

I bring home a book with a map and I show my parents where Vietnam is.

"It's thousands of miles away," I tell them.

My mom cries and my dad keeps his worry and fear inside. His smile is gone.

Coming out of a store we see a woman handing out papers talking about the war. She asks my mom in English, "Is your son in the war?" My mom looks at me and I translate.

"Yes, my Leo is in Vietnam."

"Well get ready lady, he'll be coming home in a box."

When I tell my mom what the woman said, she drops her groceries and covers her mouth with her hands to stop the sobs.

I get so angry at the woman that I kick the leg on her folding table and all the papers fall to the ground.

What used to be mom's dresser is now an altar. Candles burn day and night. Pictures of Jesus, the Virgin Mary, Saint Jude, the patron saint of difficult cases, and Leo are there.

The only place where I can pray is in my tiny closet. I go in and close the door and in the darkness I say, "I don't know if You're there or if You can hear me, but please keep my brother safe."

Mealtimes are no longer happy. Leo made us laugh with his jokes and silly stories. He'd make mom dance with him in the kitchen. "Put your mother down, she's going to burn our dinner," my dad would say.

Leo had a habit of looking at me across the table.

"Hey, Ugly," he'd say with a smile. Then he'd kick me under the table.

Many months have passed. It seems like forever. In the pit of my stomach I feel like I'm waiting for something to happen. The fear and worry makes the lines on my dad's face deeper and I can tell mom's been crying.

It's very early in the morning when the phone rings. My dad picks up the receiver. My mom insists on knowing who's calling. Right away I know it's about Leo. Is he dead? Is he hurt? No. Dad's speaking Spanish and he's smiling. The call is from Leo. He's in New Jersey and he's coming home. I run to my closet. All I can say is "thank You," over and over again.

My brother is home. He looks different, he acts different, he even smells different. He goes outside to smoke and he comes in smelling of cigarettes. He seldom smiles and he won't talk about what he's seen.

My dad says, "We need to let him be. Leave him to find his way back. He knows we love him."

Thanksgiving and Christmas are the hardest for Leo. He talks about buddies that didn't make it home. I think he feels guilty he survived.

Every night I knock on his door to say goodnight. I throw him a kiss which he doesn't return.

Mom and I take dad's advice. We don't push. But I'm always looking for signs. Time goes by and one day he picks up the sports pages. He starts watching games on TV with my dad. Maybe it's my imagination, he looks better.

My mom's putting food on the table. My dad's talking about rain in Texas.

Leo sits across from me.

"Hey, ugly," he says, and kicks me under the table.

My wonderful, goofy brother is back.

The Unexpected

Darkness came early this time of year, but it didn't stop Mae from doing what she did every day. She had enough reflective tape on her jacket, pants and even the back of her shoes to let an approaching car know she was there. A light half a mile away could illuminate her from head to toe. She had never felt unsafe or spooked, as she would say, until tonight. As she came around a clump of short trees, she started walking faster and took to the middle of the road. She turned to look back a few times and thought she saw something shine in the darkness. It could have been a stray cat or a raccoon. She became afraid when she realized there were no oncoming lights to cause the reflection, if indeed it was an animal.

She picked up her speed, raced up the

driveway and sprinted up the four steps to her porch. She locked the front door behind her and went directly to the kitchen to make sure that door was locked as well. Mae was not the type to give in to fear, yet tonight she had a feeling she had been followed.

She turned on the lights in the kitchen and hall. The lamps in the living room were already lit. She went to close the front room drapes and that's when she saw them. There were three of them. They were standing on top of a large rectangular planter. Three of them, side by side. They were peering through the large picture window. Their eyes fixed on Mae. "Oh my God," she gasped, "what do they want?"

She had seen their picture on the front pages of the tabloids, never paying much attention, but these were faces no one could forget. They were short, and had large hairless heads with big eyes, two small holes where a nose should be and a slit for a mouth. She couldn't tell what they wore because they were grey from top to bottom. Their arms were long and thin and hung almost to the ground. They carried nothing that she could see.

Mae didn't move. Very slowly she lowered her hand to her thigh and pinched it hard. She felt the pain so she must be awake, this was not a dream. The three were looking at her for what seemed like a long time. She was frozen where she stood. Her mind was racing. "I can make a run for the wall phone in the kitchen, but by the time any help arrives I could be dead."

Almost immediately after uttering those words all feelings of fear and danger left her. "I don't believe they're here to hurt me." Although they never made a sound, they were communicating with her and she knew it. She understood them.

With no regard to the consequences, she walked to the door, unlocked and opened it. "Hello," she said in a soft voice. She didn't smile, yet her face was relaxed and didn't show signs of fear. The three grey creatures hopped off the planter and walked right past her into the living room. The strange visitors again stood side by side, silent and without expression. Mae looked at them and spoke. "My name is Mae. I'm a woman. I believe you come in peace and don't mean to hurt me." She extended her hand, palm up, toward them. The creature in the middle lifted his arm, pointed a long, thin finger toward her hand and very gently touched the tip of her finger.

She waited for what seemed a long time. Perhaps they would tell her what they wanted. They appeared to be taking in the room and its contents. If one turned, the others would also follow his gaze. Mae noticed that all three appeared curious about the pictures on the table.

Mae picked up a framed picture of a young man and woman. "This is my son and his wife, I'm his mother." She picked up another one. "This is Jim, my husband; he died five years ago." The creatures didn't speak but made sounds which Mae figured was how they communicated with each other. The apparent leader of the group lifted his arm and pointed to each of the pictures and waited for Mae to explain who it was. "These are my son's children, my grandchildren, I'm their grandmother." More chattering between the three as they pointed to different frames on the table. They seemed to be intrigued, if not confused, by the ceramic cats and dogs decorating the room. As she moved to pick up a photo she made her rocking chair move which caught the attention of the trio. "It's alright," she assured them, "it's my chair, look." She sat in it and slowly rocked back and forth.

This is unbelievable, she thought. How can I tell anyone what has happened tonight? No one will believe me. I'm having trouble believing it myself.

"You must be far more intelligent than any of us on earth. Why come to me? I'm an ordinary person." The three grey beings didn't seem interested in her questions instead they continued to scan the room and its contents, though never touching anything. The one creature who appeared to be the quiet one, surprised his companions by pointing to a picture Mae hadn't explained yet. "Oh, this," she said, "these are two flowers my grandchildren gave me. We give flowers to show love." She pointed to her heart. "I keep the flowers in this frame to remember." She pointed to her head. The leader of the group stretched his arm and again pointed, this time to the door. Mae understood it was time for them to leave. The beings went out the same way they came in. Mae stood at the door and watched them walk away. They never looked back and were gone as mysteriously as they had appeared.

She woke up late, although she seldom overslept. She was still wearing her running clothes, except for her shoes which were neatly placed on the night table. Noticing what she was wearing, she talked to herself in the mirror. "Boy, I must have been tired last night or I'm really getting old. And what a strange place for my shoes!" She made a face at herself in the mirror and walked into the bathroom.

Mae felt unusually well rested and refreshed. Her mind was clear and she felt motivated to begin her daily routine. The warm water from the shower felt especially good this morning. It was at this time she started remembering the dream. "Wow!" she exclaimed to herself. "What a dream!" she laughed under her breath recalling bits and pieces of last night's strange dream.

Her routine had been the same for years. Only illness and natural disaster could alter it; put on the coffee, turn on the radio, go get the paper. On her way to the front door she noticed something on her chair. Thoughts came racing into her brain. "Last night was only a dream. It couldn't have happened," she tried to convince herself. No one could fool her, including herself. On the rocking chair were three flowers, carefully placed on the seat so she'd be sure to see them.

Mae never told a living soul about that night. As the years passed and she grew older, sometimes she almost convinced herself it had been a dream or the product of an overactive imagination. Then she would look at the frames on her picture table and there next to the flowers given to her by her grandchildren, so long ago, was a golden frame with three little flowers as proof that indeed she had received a most unexpected visit.

Lone Star Diner

Annie wasn't sure and she didn't question why she thought of the Diner as a person, not as a place. There's something to be said about simple people and places. With its coffee and bacon smell, squeaky door and worn counter, it didn't pretend to be anything else but what it was. Annie liked that. She liked the people too. She liked how Joe called everyone sweetheart, even the guys. Besides, the Diner had become a place of refuge for her. Here she felt safe.

The call came at the worst time, lunchtime and the place was packed. The phone rang several times before Joe's big arm reached from around the kitchen and grabbed the receiver off the wall.

"Yeah, yeah," he answered impatiently. "Are you sure?" His voice sounded concerned. He tossed the spatula to Fred the dish washer.

"Turn the burgers over," he ordered as he walked a few steps into the dining room. He took Annie by the arm and pulled her toward the back door.

"What's going on?" she asked.

Joe was a man of few words, he didn't know how else to tell her. "Annie, I just got a call from the oil field, there's been an accident."

Annie's eyes widened and her mouth opened but no sound came out. Joe's big hands were wrapped around her wrists, "Phil's been killed."

Annie felt her legs go weird, "Joe, Joe, what?"

"Honey, there's been a bad accident in the field, they've taken Phil to the hospital."

Joe grabbed Harry who was sitting on a stool near the back door. "Harry, take Annie to the hospital, pronto."

Annie's mind was racing. She felt numb. Harry drove as fast as he could, never saying a word. It was no secret that Phil was a real nasty piece of work. Harry's truck hadn't come to a complete stop when she jumped out and ran into the emergency room entrance.

"I'm Annie Jones, my husband Phil is here."

This day had started horribly.

"You stupid bitch!" Phil had spat out the words and without warning grabbed her by the hair and flung her against the wall. She had learned not to move from where she landed and to cover her face as best she could. Any sounds from her only made him more violent. She stayed in a heap on the floor until she heard him leave. She got up and steadied herself at the kitchen sink. She let the cold water run through her fingers, grabbed a paper towel and wiped the tears and snot from her face.

Now at the hospital, two men who worked with Phil saw Annie, and came over to where she was standing by the nurses' desk. She knew just by looking at them, Phil was dead. Maybe it was the shock, she couldn't feel anything.

"Oh my God," she murmured to herself, remembering how this morning on her way to work she kept saying over and over again, "God, please help me." Had God answered her prayer by dropping a fifty pound weight on

Phil's head? "No, of course not," she told herself. "God doesn't work that way."

She called Phil's younger brother. Bill's reaction was to sob uncontrollably when he learned of his brother's death. The hospital could hold the body for two days during which time Phil's family would make arrangements to bring him home for burial.

It seemed like a terrible nightmare, this whole thing felt unreal. Annie was trying hard to focus but her mind was jumping around and she couldn't make it stop. She went from feeling sad to being angry for feeling any sadness over a man who'd treated her so miserably. The past three years had been hell. Phil's demons came out early on and she'd borne the brunt of his violence. Right now she needed to be still, remind herself she didn't have to be afraid any longer and let the dust settle.

A week after Phil got killed she emptied the closet of his clothes. She threw away all his shaving stuff, toothbrush, and anything else that was his. She moved the furniture around, changed the position of the bed and opened all the windows to let air in. The forgiving and forgetting would take time but she knew it would eventually come. In the meantime she'd get out of bed each morning, put one foot in front of the other and do what she needed to do. She'd been on her own for a long time before meeting Phil, she could do it again.

The knock on the door jarred her back to reality.

"Who is it?" she asked.

"Annie, I've brought Phil's car. It was left at work all this time."

She had forgotten all about it. Since she didn't drive, the car hadn't been important.

"Just put it in the tenants' parking, please."

"I'll bring you back the key," said the voice through the closed door.

Annie returned to work at the Lone Star Diner. Nothing there had changed. Joe was still hollering when food was ready for pick up. The same people were ordering the same things. Although everyone knew, very few said anything about Phil's death. Joe and Fred were especially nice to her.

"Your hair sure looks pretty, hon," commented Jill, the other waitress. The guys who worked at the factory left a little extra tip on the table. These small kindnesses didn't go unnoticed by Annie. She felt safe and loved. She was glad to be back.

The customers were gone and the end-of-the-day chores were almost done. Joe came out of the kitchen with two glasses of iced tea.

"Here you go, girls, take a break."

The radio in the kitchen was playing a sweet country song. Annie hummed along. She sat at her favorite place near the backdoor. From here she could see the mountains in the distance, a sight that always lifted her spirit. She walked over to the wall where people tacked up handwritten pieces of paper offering free puppies, tires for sale, rooms for rent. She knew the one she was looking for. It hadn't meant much before but now she had to find it. Here was a chance to move forward in more ways than one. She felt a renewed sense of excitement. A broad smile came on her face as she pulled the piece of paper from the wall. It read:

CLAIM YOUR FREEDOM -
LEARN TO DRIVE!!!

Stardust Trailer Park

The arch proudly announced the entrance to The Stardust Trailer Park. Pale blue neon letters with three stars that blinked on and off. At night it cast a lovely light on the well-manicured road that meandered through the park.

Now with years of neglect taking its toll, the stars were the first to go out. Then one by one the letters went out so the sign which originally read
       THE STARDUST TRAILER PARK
became
       THE _TARDUST TRAILER PARK
and the final blow was when the sign read
       THE _ _ _ _ DUST TRA_ _ _ _ P_ _ _

The whining of the neon hummed off tune until, with what seemed like a great sigh, the sign completely went out. There was no money for repairs. With sadness, Mike the manager, opened the electrical box and turned it off for good.

The Stardust Trailer Park had become a repository of old people in old trailers. With no money or energy to spare, no one painted or fixed the trailers which sat on neglected patches of brown grass.

It was shortly after the sign went out that an unusual electrical storm with thunder and lighting came through. Unusual for this part of Southern California where rain alone can create a panic in TV weathermen and cause traffic jams on the freeways for hours.

The thunder seemed to echo and bounce off the metal sides of the trailers and the lighting cast eerie shadows. The wind whipped the rain and then the electricity went out. Mike grabbed his flashlight, and from his window he could see a few lights appear as other residents turned their flashlights on as well.

Mike was startled by the loud knock on his trailer door. He didn't want any of the old people wondering around in the dark. He pulled the door open and to his surprise it was a young woman, a pretty blond girl in her early twenties, dressed in white. In the light from his flashlight he thought she looked like an angel.

Without waiting to be asked, she came inside. "I'm Mrs. Ryan's granddaughter."

"She's in the hospital," Mike responded

"Yes I know, she wanted me to come and check on her place and stay here until she returns."

Mike fidgeted with his flashlight. He tried not to shine it directly into the girl's face. "The lights are out because of the storm, they should come back soon, do you want to wait here?"

"No," the girl replied. "I have the key and I'll let myself in and wait there." Mike didn't take his eyes off her as she walked to her grandmother's trailer and disappeared inside.

Later that night, when the lights came back, Mike walked around the park looking for broken tree branches and runaway trash cans. He kept thinking about the girl. He didn't hear a taxi or a car dropping her off. He wondered how she'd gotten here.

The question nagged Mike, but he didn't want to come straight out and ask the young woman how she'd gotten there, or how it was that she knew exactly which was Mrs. Ryan's trailer.

The storm moved on to places east and the morning was bright and beautiful. Mike kept an eye out and when he saw her walking toward the street, he hurried out and waved hello.

"Hi there," he said. "Was everything okay at your Grandma's?"

"Yes, thanks," she replied.

"With all the excitement of the storm I didn't tell you, I'm Mike, the park manager." He extended his hand.

"I'm sorry," she smiled, "I didn't even tell you my name. I'm Angie. I have to catch the bus; see you later." She waved as she ran to the bus stop.

Mike seemed satisfied with the little information he'd been able to get. Angie was dressed in white and on her way to work.

Not much thought was given to the girl in Mrs. Ryan's trailer. The Stardust Trailer Park had its share of cranky, tired and lonely people. Battles over stupid things created factions and cliques which changed over time, and there was always someone who didn't like someone and if you asked why they couldn't tell you because they'd forgotten.

Without the old folks realizing it, a new sense of calm settled over the decrepit place. Angie didn't care that some of her neighbors were grumpy and mean. She just kept on doing the things that she felt needed to be done. She'd roll out the trash cans, pick up milk and bread at the store for the housebound, and always said hello even when she was ignored.

Little by little changes happened. Fran started to nod at her when greeted. Clem begrudgingly threw away the shoes he couldn't tie and accepted the new pair with Velcro. Angie's patience and sweet nature were noticed and appreciated by some of the old people.

Angie's schedule was the same each day. She left for work in the morning and returned by 5:00 p.m. No one asked her what she did. She was comfortable with this lack of interest; it meant she didn't have to give too many details.

"Hi, Peggy," Angie would call across the brown grass patch. "Do you need anything from the store?"

The old people, used to being ignored, noticed and liked the attention Angie gave them. Some of the old ladies would let her hold their hands. People seemed to be more alert. Almost as though they were waking up from a long slumber.

"You have the most beautiful white hair," were the words Myrtle needed to hear to prompt her to comb it. Joe took a shower. Fred found his teeth and was eloquent as he told the story of being present at the raising of the flag on Iwo Jima. No one knew this about Fred. He walked a bit taller after that. Pete returned Joe's hammer he'd borrowed two years ago and after many years Mary waved hello to Sarah.

The postage-size squares of grass were getting watered and a few plastic flowers found their way into long abandoned pots.

"Mike, what's up with the sign?" asked Angie. "I bet its pretty when its lit up."

"It hasn't worked for a long time," Mike answered. "I finally just turned it off for good."

"Where's the switch?"

"Come on Angie," Mike argued. "I'm telling you, the thing is dead."

Angie didn't give up and walked to the small utility shed where the electrical box was located. He hurried behind her. Not to stop her, but to make sure she didn't get electrocuted. Angie opened the lid of the box and found the word "sign" written in black next to a switch.

Angie flipped the switch and nothing happened.

Mike and Angie craned their necks as they looked out the small window. A small flicker on the far corner of the sign startled them. Mike was waiting for the whole thing to go up in flames, Angie was optimistic.

A pale blue star began to materialize. Then another. The letter "S" lit up. Mike and Angie held hands and jumped up and down, screaming each time a segment of the neon came to life.

People began to come out of their trailers. Some in nightclothes and robes. They hurried to the sign like tattered moths attracted by the pale blue light.

"It's a miracle," said Sarah.

"No!" argued Fred. "The damn thing just had time to rest."

It didn't matter. The sign was lit and it was beautiful.

The old people looked forward to dusk when Mike would turn it on. Some dragged their lawn chairs and sat on a grassy patch to enjoy the light. Angie passed around a box of graham crackers and Mike supplied the lemonade in small paper cups.

The always present feeling of anger and annoyance had dissipated. More greetings were exchanged. Oscar brought out his ukulele and several joined him in an off-key singalong. Laughter, something not heard in a long time, was a welcome sound.

"Hang on," Mike shouted toward the

door. "I'm coming."

Mike opened the door to two people he had never seen before. The man began to speak. Mike's face looked like he'd been slapped. The couple noticed his shock and disbelief. "No sir," the man said. "We don't have a niece. My mother doesn't know a girl named Angie."

"You must be wrong. She's Mrs. Ryan's granddaughter. This girl has been living in your mom's trailer for months now," Mike said.

"Listen mister, I should know who our relations are and this girl is not my mother's granddaughter or my niece or anything," said Mrs. Ryan's son. "Do you have a key to my mom's place? We need to go in and check it out."

Mrs. Ryan's daughter-in-law never said a word. She kept her hand on her husband's arm and patted it whenever he raised his voice and his face turned red.

Mike walked them to the trailer and used his key to let them in. They walked inside not knowing what to expect.

"The place sure looks a lot cleaner than when your mom was here," said the woman.

Her husband threw her a disapproving look.

"Can you tell if anything is missing?" asked Mike.

"Not really, Mom didn't have anything of value, just her TV and some books and it seems like they're all here. We're just going to sit here and wait for this girl to come then we'll all know what the hell's been going on."

"Are you going to call the police?" asked Mike.

"I don't know. I suppose it depends on her and what she has to say."

With thoughts racing in his head, Mike sat by the window all afternoon waiting for Angie to return. Had he been taken in by a scammer? Was this girl a thief or worse yet, a criminal? He was so confused and afraid of what was going to happen. All he knew was that Angie was a sweet friendly girl, good to everyone and never asked for anything in return. Time seemed to slow down to a crawl. The Ryans waited inside the trailer and Mike kept his vigil at the window.

Shortly after 5:30 Mike saw Angie walk into the park. He wanted to run out and warn her and perhaps she would tell him it was all a big mistake and things would be alright again, but he didn't move. He watched as she went inside the trailer. The lights were on and he could see the three people inside. Mike was praying the police wouldn't be called, not only for Angie's sake but for the old people who were rattled so easily.

Mike pulled his door open before Angie had a chance to knock.

"Angie, what in God's name is going on? Are these people crazy?"

Her eyes were red from crying and tears were still running down her cheeks.

"Mike, I'm so very sorry. I never meant to hurt anyone."

"Are you telling me these people are right?" asked Mike.

Angie wiped her eyes.

"I took the key from Mrs. Ryan's handbag at the nursing home."

"But you had never been here before, how did you know which was her trailer?"

"It was the angel," she said.

"What angel?"

"The one that's hanging by the front door. Mrs. Ryan told me it was a guardian angel and it took care of anyone who lived in the trailer."

Mike looked devastated.

"Did you think no one would catch on? Are they going to call the police?"

"No. They just want me to get out right now."

He didn't want her to go, yet there was nothing he could do.

Angie walked out of the trailer park that night as silently as she had arrived.

For a while, after she had left, people asked where she'd gone. As time passed they stopped asking.

Things would undoubtedly return to how they were before Angie came, but for now, Mike turned on the sign and the old folks came out of their trailers and sat under the pale blue neon light.

John Wayne Wears a Girdle

I'm scared to go into the principal's office. Any moment now the lady behind the desk will call my name and I'll have to go in. I know he's going to be angry. Once before I was sent to him for calling a girl a bad name. She started it and it ended with me getting detention. I'm glad we don't have a phone. They can't call my mom; the office lady will give me a note to take home and I'll translate it for my mom who will look disappointed and give me the lecture about being a widow and not having my dad to help raise me. Oh, boy.

I want to tell you my side of the story and have you decide if that stupid George didn't deserve the punch in the nose.

I save every penny I get my hands on.

I sell bottles, run errands. I even don't buy the little boxes of chocolate milk at school. I save my money so I can go to the movies. My favorites are the cowboy movies, and I love John Wayne. I make sure I have money for the bus and my ticket. If I'm lucky and my mom gives me a dime I can buy a hot dog that comes in the foil bag that keeps the bun warm and soft. I love The Majestic Theater. It's beautiful. Two balconies, thick carpets, royal blue velvet curtains that open just before the movie starts, and if you look up, there are twinkling lights in the ceiling that look like stars. I don't like to sit in the balconies. That's where couples go to smooch. I also don't like to sit next to people who talk during the show. I find my seat, I curl my legs under me and I wait for the lights to go down and the movie to begin.

On Mondays we always ask each other, "Did you go to the show?" We don't call them movies or films. If someone says, "I'm going to the show," we know what it means.

On Saturday afternoon I take the bus, buy my show ticket and sit by myself. Once the show starts I forget everything including that my dad died last year and that we have no money, and that the perm I got from my mom makes me look like a fat Shirley Temple. Sitting in the dark watching the show is heaven to me. Yes, I do love John Wayne. Not like you love a boyfriend but how you feel about someone who's good, kind and strong. I like him so much that I root for him even if it means the Mexicans get killed.

I imagine John Wayne's kids are the luckiest in the world. He's tall, good-looking and brave. No one messes with him.

So now, let me tell you why I'm sitting here waiting for the principal. It wasn't my fault. Stupid George started it all.

"Hey Gorda, I saw you at the show on Saturday. Girls aren't suppose to like cowboy movies. What's wrong with you anyhow?"

I ignore him. I sit at my desk but I can still hear him telling other boys I like cowboy movies and they're all giggling. During lunch he comes over to bug me again.

"Hey Gorda, you're in love with John Wayne. You want to marry him."

"No I don't and you're just stupid."

"Then how come you tell everyone he's your favorite movie star?"

"Because he's the best and if you knew anything you would know that."

"Here's something you don't know. My sister read it in a movie magazine and it said that John Wayne wears a girdle."

Everyone in the lunch room hears stupid George and they start laughing. I feel my face get hot and the next thing I know I have my fist in his face and blood is running out of his nose.

119

The lunch room lady runs over and puts a kitchen towel on his face and takes him away crying.

You know you're in trouble when the principal starts with, "Well young lady."

"We sent George home with a bloody nose and now I want to know why you hit him?"

"He said something terrible to me. I didn't mean to make his nose bleed. I just wanted him to stop saying those awful things."

A look of concern comes over Mr. Johnson's face.

"What did he say to you to make you this upset that you had to hit him?"

"It's so awful I don't know if I can say it to you."

"Will you feel better telling Mrs. Brown, and she can tell me?"

"No. It's a terrible thing no matter who I tell it to."

"What did George say to you? If it's truly that bad I will deal with him."

I put my hands over my face. I know I have to repeat those ugly words which have to be a lie.

"John Wayne wears a girdle," I mumbled through my fingers.

"I'm sorry, but can you repeat that?"

"He said John Wayne wears a girdle," I repeated in a loud voice.

I break into tears. I'm not sure if it's because I'm still so angry or because I know I'm in trouble with the principal.

Mr. Johnson comes from around his desk and hands me some Kleenex and touches my shoulder. For a moment I think I see the corner of his mouth curl up in a grin.

"I suppose you were very angry and felt you had to hurt him back."

I nodded.

"You know I can't have students hitting each other. No matter what. You can always come to me and I will take care of whatever is going on. I'm afraid you have to stay in detention for a week and write a note apologizing to George."

When I get home I hand my mom the note from the principal's office.

"Here," she hands it back to me, "tell me what it says."

I have to think fast. A new cowboy show is coming to the Aztec Theater on Saturday and I don't want to miss it.

I read the note slowly and carefully.

Dear Mrs. Garcia,
        This is to let you know that your daughter has volunteered to help after school for the next five days. She's a helpful girl. And knows western history real well.
                                Sincerely,
                                The Principal

Tillie and Ted

Tia Tillie was buried today. The funeral was short and sweet. My sister Pat and her husband came from Galveston. Three women from Tillie's apartment building came to the church. It was nice of them to come. After the burial Pat, her husband and I went to Denny's for lunch. The three women didn't come, they had other things to do. I think it's very nice of my cousin Norma to send flowers, especially since she didn't even know Tia Tillie.

When we were teenagers, all the cousins were curious about Tillie. All her pictures were either hidden or thrown away. The bits and pieces that we heard only made us want to know more. What could she have done that was so terrible that the family disowned her. My grandmother, Tillie's sister, and my mom spoke in hushed tones as though there was a terrible secret. Shortly before my grandmother died, I got up the nerve to ask her about her sister one more time.

"Grandma, don't you think we're old enough and it's about time we knew about Tillie? It's hard for me to imagine what she could have done to make the family despise her."

"Tillie was the prettiest of all the sisters and different in many ways. She smoked, she drank, she did wild things that good girls just didn't do. If one sister had a bad reputation, people assumed they were all the same. We pleaded and we fought with her, but she wouldn't change. Then she met a man. She knew that he would never be accepted but she chose him over us. She didn't give a damn about her family."

"What was so bad about this man that the family objected so strongly?"

"He was a Negro." I could hear the anger in my grandmother's voice.

"Grandma, you mean his only crime was that he was black?"

"Yes. A black soldier from Louisiana. It's all so different now. No one cares who you marry but back then it was asking for trouble - bad trouble - especially in Texas where lynchings were still happening."

I swallowed hard. I didn't know what to say. I was torn between what was true for that time and the injustice of the whole situation. I never mentioned Tillie to my grandmother again.

It was in December of 2005 that I got the call. Not in a million years did I expect this.

"Hello, this is Tillie Lopez, are you Maria's daughter?"

I immediately recognized the name. "Yes, I'm Julie. Are you my Aunt Tillie?"

"Yes, it's me. I'm sorry I didn't come to your mom's funeral, I heard she died. I remember her as a sweet girl."

"You didn't come for my grandmother's funeral either," I said.

"No I didn't. I didn't think she wanted me there."

"Tia, are you calling from Louisiana or are you here in Houston?"

"I'm back and I would like to see you, if it's alright with you."

I hung up the phone and sat for a long time thinking of reasons why Tillie would call now after so many years.

When I got to the address she'd given me I realized it was a seniors' apartment building. I knocked on the door and a tall, good-looking older woman answered. Her white hair was in a bun and she wore a pale blue pant suit. You could tell she was a beauty in her youth. She greeted me with a handshake. I was relieved. I didn't know if I should hug her, being that we were total strangers.

I took the beer she offered me and we tried, as she put it, to "Readers Digest" her story.

"There used to be juke joints on the outskirts of town then. The best black musicians would come to play. Very few Mexicans went there and every once in a while white musicians would come to listen to the music. That's where I met Ted. He was the handsomest man I'd ever seen. He was still wearing his Army uniform, it was 1945 and he was waiting to be discharged."

She looked at me to see my reaction. "Did my sister tell you he was black?"

"Yes, once when I pressed her to tell me about you."

She continued. "At first we only met where no one knew us. When it became serious I went to my family and it was World War II all over again. They demanded I stop seeing him. They threatened to have Ted arrested. I don't know what for, since I was over twenty-one. I made my choice and I went with Ted."

I sat mesmerized as my great-aunt talked about her life. She did it with such ease. She had nothing to hide and nothing to be ashamed of.

"Ted and I left Houston and drove an old beat up car all the way to New Orleans. We got married by a justice of the peace. The old guy assumed I was Creole because of my Hispanic last name or maybe he just didn't care. We rented a small apartment in one of the black neighborhoods. The landlady was concerned that I was not black. But Ted made up a story that I was part Mexican, part Native American and part light skin black. She was okay with that and we lived there for a long time. Ted teased me about passing for black. We were so happy then. Ted and I ran a little joint where we served hot food. Ted had been an Army cook, you know, and he was very good at it. Soon we had more customers and we moved to a bigger place. He was the sweetest man I'd ever met; he was a wonderful husband and I miss him everyday. We didn't have kids but we had each other. My family didn't want to have anything to do with me. The first few years I'd sent Christmas and birthday cards and they'd be returned to me unopened."

"When the cousins and I got together we used to talk about you, look at us now, I never thought I'd meet you."

Tia Tillie had been gone for almost

sixty-five years. Her sisters were all dead. The family had shrunk to a few nieces and their kids. To be honest, only a few of us still remembered her and we thought she was dead.

"I'm very happy you called me but I'm curious why now after all these years?"

"I'm old and I can't last too much longer. I suppose I just wanted to connect with someone 'de mi sangre' (of my blood)." A look of sadness came over her face.

"I feel like Sherlock Holmes, finally unraveling the mystery of Tillie." I hoped my bad joke lightened the mood.

"We sold the café in 1990 and we planned to travel but Ted was sick already. He died in 1995. We ran the café for forty years. Can you imagine! No one could believe how many people came to Ted's funeral. He knew so many people and everyone loved him. I planned to stay in New Orleans for the rest of my life and then I started getting lonesome for home. After all these years I was homesick. Hard to believe, isn't it? I'm sure it's just old age but I said, 'what the hell, go back if that's what you want.' I like these apartments and the people are friendly. I'm happy here."

She looked at me, "Will you come and visit me again?"

"Let someone try and stop me," I said.

Tia Tillie and I became friends. My daughter and my grandkids came to meet her. My sister Pam, who lives in Galveston, came to visit also. I made it a habit to see her once a week and we always had lots to talk about.

One day she said to me, "Go in my closet and bring the small metal box."

In it were pictures of her and Ted. She was so beautiful and he was so handsome. There were pictures of the café, Mardi Gras parties, fishing trips and the two of them kissing next to a Christmas tree.

I knew Tillie wasn't well. I continued my visits the same as before.

"I've been waiting for you," she'd say the moment I walked through the door.

"You didn't forget did you?" she asked.

I'd reach into my handbag and pull out a brown bag with a cold can of beer. Her eyes lit up when I yanked on the pull-tab and handed her the can.

"I have something else for you I think you'll like," I said. I gave her a small wrapped package and she tore it open like it was Christmas morning.

"Oh, honey, this is beautiful. Look at my Ted, he's so handsome."

I had taken one of her pictures and framed it so she could keep it by her bedside.

Tia Tillie never complained although she got worse. Near the end I would sit beside her and hold her hand.

"I'm not afraid to die. I believe I'll see Ted again - and I can't wait."

Tia Tillie was buried today. I know I'll miss her. I put her and Ted's picture on my mantle next to pictures of my Grandmother, my Mom and Dad and other family members.

The other day someone asked, "Who are the people in that picture?"

"That my Tia Tillie and my Uncle Ted. Aren't they a great looking couple?"

I Remember the Alamo

I love and hate summer. I love it because there's no school. I hate it because it's so hot in the day and still hot at night. On some nights my mom uses a cardboard to fan me with because I can't fall asleep. I've seen pictures in magazines of places where kids play in a lake or by a river, and they look so cool. I don't mean cool - as in cool cats - I mean not sweating and itchy with prickly rash.

I look at the calendar on the kitchen wall and mark the days as they pass. July 1, 1954 - that's today. It's the first of the month and our Social Security checks come in the mail. My mom goes to Jimmy's to cash them, it's the nearest grocery store. It's owned by a Chinese man everyone calls Jimmy, I bet that's not his real name. My mom gives me money for the bus and three dimes for me to spend any way I want. I'll probably buy a cold soda and a bag of Fritos.

I take the bus that says 'Prospect Hill' on the window. People rush in to get a seat. Men in uniform from the Air Force base usually sit in the back. They sound happy. They talk loud and laugh with each other. They're glad to go to town. Old ladies with bunches of flowers from their gardens are going to the big church for a special rosary. I look at the people and I try to imagine how they live. Are they happy? Do they have nice children? Or do they worry about money like my mom?

I wonder why it says 'Prospect Hill' when it's coming and going. It should say 'Downtown.' Anyway, it doesn't matter because I know where I'm going. I'm going to The Alamo. They say it's a shrine but I don't see any saints. The Alamo has lots of rooms. Some with pictures along the walls and others have canons and old rifles and guns. I go from room to room. No one bothers me. There's only one old man at the entrance and either he doesn't see me or he thinks I'm with the other people coming in. People come from all around to visit. The dads like to look at the rifles and guns. The moms stop to read everything that's up on the walls, the kids look bored.

I find this is the best place to play. I didn't find it by myself. My best friend Rosie and I found it together. It doesn't cost to come in. She and I come here a lot. We like it better than the park where there's little shade and too many people. She's gone now. Rosie and her family go to 'las piscas' in places like Michigan to pick fruit in the summer. The whole family goes in a big truck. The mom and dad sit up front and all the kids ride in the back of the truck, they sit on mattresses and pillows. I miss Rosie. Last year she sent me a postcard with a picture of a lake. I had never received mail before.

I go to the very back, behind the buildings, near the stone wall where it's shady. I have found a way of climbing on the wall and walking almost the whole way around. There are no guards telling me to, "get off," or, "don't jump around." When I'm in the big rooms where the flags and the pictures of the dead are, I'm very quiet and don't touch anything. 'Please Do Not Touch' signs are on the canons and the old wooden carts outside. Some people don't read or don't care, they sit on the carts, smile big toothy grins and take pictures of each other.

Last year in fifth grade we studied all about The Alamo and the battle between the Texans and the Mexicans. It seems that The Alamo was an old abandoned place to begin with so I had trouble understanding why everyone was in such a hurry to die for it. I think our teacher felt bad having to tell us over and over again how the Mexicans killed every single person here. All us kids in the class are Mexican and maybe she thinks some of our relatives were in Santa Anna's army.

I feel bad for Davy Crockett. I used to watch him on my aunt's TV.

When we go to the cemetery to visit my grandma and my dad I'm told to be quiet and don't run around stepping on the graves. All the men at The Alamo died in one night. There are no grave stones here. I guess they were buried somewhere else. Sometimes I sit under the trees where it's cool, back by the stone wall, and think of the people who died here. In every battle in my history book people die. I wonder if they get together in heaven and talk about it?

I spend hours playing here. Today two blond kids hang around with me and I play teacher. I take them to see the old rifles and guns. I show them my favorite place, way back where the tree branches touch the ground and I play it's my hideout. We go to the drinking fountain and fill our mouths with cool water and squirt each other. A man wearing a cowboy hat tells us to stop being silly. We laugh and run away. This is my favorite place. I come here when it's hot. I feel quiet here. I think most people find it quiet too. They look and point to things but they never yell. I suppose it isn't polite to yell when you're in a shrine.

I walk several blocks to the bus stop. I can see the Prospect Hill bus is almost here. I ride to the end of the line which is 24th street. Everyone gets out. People go in different directions. They remind me of cockroaches, the way they scatter. I still have my three dimes. I go to the little store and buy a bottle of Hippo grape soda. Cokes taste better but the Hippo bottle is really big and costs the same. I wait for the shuttle bus that takes me to the stop across from my house. It's too hot to walk When I get home my mom's in the kitchen. "Where did you go?" she asks.

"The Alamo," I tell her.

"What in the world do you do there? Do they just let you in?"

"Yes," I answer. "The old man at the door lets everyone in. It's a shrine, you know."

She just says, "Hummm," and keeps stirring the pot.

I look for my fifth grade history book and read about The Alamo again. Too bad the story always ends the same.

Gone

After forty-eight years I came back, back to the city with the river and bad memories. No family and no friends, no reason to return. Memories of poverty and prejudice, like gate guards, kept me away.

I said to John, my husband, "I'm grown up, I can take coming back."

"I hope so," he replied.

We drove down my street, a street I knew so well.

"You've gone too far, turn around," I insisted.

The house where I grew up, the house

my father built was gone. My grandmother's house was gone. The house and orchard beyond that was gone too. All gone.

Not trying to be mean, John reminded me, "You've been away almost fifty years, what did you expect?"

He was right.

The only house that looked half-way cared for was Miss Harriet's. A spinster lady who took care of her brother, an old priest who'd lost his mind. "Father Joe's not coo-coo," she would say, "he old, that's all."

"Do you think she still lives there?" John asked. "No way! She'd be over a hundred," I said.

I'd been gone a long time yet in my mind this place hadn't changed. In my mind I carried the image of the last time I saw it.

The whole neighborhood now looked like a neglected, dirty child. Lawns were dried up and houses needed paint. Roofs sagged over porches like drooping old eyelids. The early heat spell and humidity added to my discomfort. That evening, in the hotel, John asked for the second time.

"Are you okay?"

"Yes, of course I'm okay," I lied. I wasn't okay.

The next morning we got to the airport before sunrise and it was already hot and humid. As we waited for the plane that would bring us home I became aware the sadness I felt before had been replaced by a feeling of ease.

Home was where I was going, not where I was leaving.